TOUCHED BY THE ROCK

Newfoundland as Heard Through Tales And Sounds of Poems

By

James Rogin

This book is a work of non-fiction. Names and places have been changed to protect the privacy of all individuals. The events and situations are true.

© 2003 by James Rogin. All rights reserved.

No part of this book may be reproduced, stored in a retrieval system, or transmitted by any means, electronic, mechanical, photocopying, recording, or otherwise, without written permission from the author.

ISBN: 1-4107-7152-0 (e-book)
ISBN: 1-4107-7153-9 (Paperback)

This book is printed on acid free paper.

1stBooks - rev. 09/23/03

The incidents depicted in these stories and poems are true in so far as they have been related to me. However the names, dialogue and subjects are a product of my imagination. The opinions stated are mine alone. But then I am the stranger.

Picture Me This

Paint me a picture, painter man.

Paint me a picture to show

The blue waters like my ladylove's eyes,

Whose icy depths I cannot touch.

Don't give me the blue of skies above,

But the grey sullen days like company lost

In far-off multi-colored lands.

Paint for me, painter man.

Color for me, painter man.

Color the picture to show

The colors of people as they ply their trade,

Going from door to door but never seeing

The myriad colors of flowers or swaying trees

Nestled in earthy hues all along

The endless lanes, roads and yellowed concrete
walks.
Color me this, painter man.

Draw me a picture, painter man.
Draw me a picture to show
Musical notes rising in the air, bouncing from
sullen clouds.
Note the dancers in contorted gestured forms,
Making points for representation,
While in home galleries hangs the evidence
Of what is seen and heard or felt within the
heart.
Draw for me, painter man.

Sketch me a picture, painter man.
Sketch the picture to show
The beauty of cities but not the hurts

Of the poor, the hungry and jobless searching,
To labor not here but other places,

While jail houses harbor the grim
And the evil overall.
Sketch me this, painter man.

Frame me a picture, painter man.
Frame me a picture I can see.
Surround it with pine, birch and fir,
And oil the wood from the riches of the sea.
Stretch paper gained from the bounty of the
land,
And mat it in kind just as well.
From gnarled hands include the sweat and
labor
That puts it together.
Frame this for me, painter man.

Hang this picture of Newfoundland.

Hang it for the world to see,

Both the ugliness and beauty of this far-off land

So all will know

That we are not perfect. And this is so

For this is heaven's way, and if blindly we must follow,

Then hang this picture for me, painter man.

I am the stranger, the alien, and the foreigner. I have no roots, no heritage here in this land; this mountainous land that has risen out of the North Atlantic, carpeted with wild flowers and unending green trees. And every harbor has its village and every village has its tales. Tales by which you can trace a rich history and a rich culture that can make you smile and also make you cry.

I, an only child, have had the good fortune of an inheritance of a Newfoundland wife with ten siblings who became my in-laws. Thus, I now can wrap an arm around my "bro" and hug my sister. Best of all I can listen to the tales, listen to the songs, and feel the poetry of this magical and mystical land. And if I were to recount any story, I would choose one

with some sardonic twist, such as the tale of
what happened to my wife's father many years
ago.

The Triumph of Guile

The stories about the rum smugglers with their fast boats, of their escapades, are well known, but little is told of the men who work their jobs with the ferry and now and then bring back a little contraband. And even less is said of the passengers. Such is the case for a rider called Joe. A tall rangy man, he plied the ferry that sailed to St. Pierre and Miquelon, two islands that belong to France and lie just off the southern coast of the Rock. Many a man would bring back more than his allotted share of rum into Newfoundland, and most often a turn of the head or the wink of an eye would assure a safe passage for these illicit bottles.

But that arrangement changed drastically one day. I think that the "higher ups" of the company must have said something to the captain, who in turn said something to the men who worked the vessel and also to the travelers. He even went one step further, and that was to search the gear and boxes of all who boarded the ship. It wasn't long before Joe came to the vessel toting a large-sized box upon his shoulder.

"What do you have in the box?" asked the captain.

"Nothin'," Joe replied as he tried to push past the officer.

"Hold on now. I want to see what's in that box."

"Ain't nothin' but me cat."

"Now I ain't believin' that. Just you open that box."

"If I was to do that, sure me cat will run away and I'll never be able to explain that to the missus."

"I don't care about that. I'm tellin' you to open that box."

"All right. I'll open it, but if me cat escapes, I'll be blamin' you and I will want to go back ashore to find him."

"Aye me son, and if that cat does get away I'll let you go after 'im."

With that, Joe opened the box. The straggly orange striped cat jumped out, landed on the deck and stopped long enough to adjust its eyes to the light before running around the deck followed by two big men. The cat would never have left if those two behemoths hadn't been yelling, "Here kitty, kitty," and chased it about, creating a ruckus. Dodging between the legs of the men, the cat leapt off the ship and was last seen running down the wharf.

"Now see what you done. You let me cat escape. I told you that would happen and you didn't believe me. I just got to get me cat 'cause me wife will never forgive me."

"Lard Jesus, me son, I'm really sorry about that. Now you go after that mangy cat, but be back within the hour 'cause you know we'll be castin' off."

Joe went off with that big empty box upon his shoulder, looking for the nearest liquor emporium to fill it up with bottles of rum. His mission was accomplished in short order. Next, he made sure not to return too early. He took his time looking in shop windows, stopped for a quaff of beer and returned to the ship just minutes before the ferry cast off. The captain, who was waiting impatiently, spied his man and yelled for him to hurry.

"'Tis all right, Captain. I found me cat." Joe yelled back.

"Get aboard then. I'm glad you found her," the captain answered.

Joe hefts his box on his shoulder again, walks up the gangplank and salutes the captain.

"Do you want to look in me box, Captain?"

"No, me son! I don't want to go through that again, and we ain't got the time. Anyhow I'm glad you got 'er back."

So once again the average man has triumphed and has gotten one better on the system that makes a good citizen, for that one moment, a felon. Oh, what cageyness dwells within the heart of the Newfoundlander, and who else can pull off a better prank?

Dynamics of Din

When talking with my new relations, I am filled with awe at how far back in time they can trace their ancestry. What is really amazing is that they can recall names and dates practically back to Adam and Eve. They love to tell stories about other members of the family, and they have great debates about the points of the story and what it means. There seems to be only two topics to argue: one is politics and the other is family. I don't imagine all households hold court in the kitchen, but this seems to be the arena for all the great debates and telling of tales in the family into which I married. Why is it that some people seem to think that to win an argument you must talk ten decibels louder than the opponent each time you speak?

Nevertheless, this is a game with certain rules. No one interrupts the other speaker, but each must make a valid point, and each speaker in turn must raise the decibel level. It is only when the glasses begin to tremble or someone cedes the point that silence is restored. And the sudden quiet hushes everyone. Everyone simply looks at each other, then they shrug and it all begins again. But for that one moment the feeling of peace and quiet, however momentary, seems unique and wonderful.

A Tale of the Night

One tale frequently told at the kitchen table involves a brother who was a hellion as a young man. This tale is a salute to the meanness of young men and their relationship with elders.

Squid, that denizen of the deep, provides not only food but can also serve as an instrument of torture in the hands of young men. Certain unscrupulous young men, anyway.

As in many coastal towns, a river runs down to the ocean nearby in this particular town, and in many areas freshwater ponds often form behind the barrier of the beach. On warm days, children would swim in the icy ocean and then run across the beach and jump into the freshwater pond to get warm. A pathway made by the feet of many was on the other side of the pond opposite the beach.

Mrs. Buzzy was extremely superstitious. She was coming back from Sunday night services at the Salvation Army. It was well past dusk and the ebony darkness of a Newfoundland night was coming on. Knowing Mrs. Buzzy would be coming down the road, the hellions waited for her with fiendish glee. When the victim arrived, the boys held up the glowing squid to frighten the poor woman. She saw her chance to escape and started down the pathway, intent on crossing to the other side of the pond. As Mrs. Buzzy started down the path, the scurvy band raced down the beach to the place where the path ended and held the old squid on high. The squid, emitting a ghostly glow, frightened the old woman, and she turned and ran in the other direction to circumvent the apparition. But the young fiends quickly ran to the other end and once again performed that ghostly ritual. And once again, the old lady turned and went the other way. This went on until the woman was exhausted and crying for help. It was only the presence of newcomers on the scene that brought an end to the ordeal, and the scalawags scattered in different directions. The family still talks about this and laughs, but I wonder what was so humorous about this situation. Still, when you think about some of the troubles our young people get into today, I would applaud this event by comparison and proclaim it mild mischief.

Tricksters

Why do we play tricks upon each other?
Why do we cause grief and be a bother?

Why must we be the cause of hurt
For those we think are of little worth?

Then we laugh and talk for many days
And revel in our evil ways.

Why must we scourge the neighborhood?
Why do we not work for the common good?

Are we so strong when we beat the weak?
When love and kindness is all they seek.

When it comes our time to bear the taunts
Will we remember our wicked haunts?

Will we be able to understand

Those who have the upper hand?

You see the adage still holds true.

You do for others and they do for you.

The Poor Lost Soul

Poor Mrs. Buzzy! There is an often told story about her husband, about how his death had a direct impact on her feelings and emotions regarding things of the supernatural. She had lost her husband some time before the squid incident, and one of the superstitions that still exists among us today was uppermost in her mind.

On the fateful day of his passing, Mr. Buzzy had chores to do. He had set traps cross-country, which is how the locals say that he was going across the barrens. This is the type of country that can be partly bog with sinkholes and partly rocky and dry. At that time there was no paved road going across the barrens, so he had to follow an old track that may have been an Indian trail at one time. As I've been told, this was during the winter and he was probably checking to see if he had gotten any rabbits.

After hitching up his horse to the sleigh, he set out. That was the last time anyone would see him alive again. When he didn't return, Mrs. Buzzy informed her neighbors and friends. She was very concerned because it had started snowing and that could be very dangerous out on the barrens. Oh how they searched and searched, but Mr. Buzzy was never found.

It was not until four years later that a hunter found Mr. Buzzy, or rather his bones. He was in a sitting position at the base of a tree, and the bones of his horse were there as well, tied to the tree as if the ghostly remainder of that horse might still gallop away.

No one knows for sure what happened, but some people guess that he had a heart attack and sat down to rest after managing to tie the horse. If Mr. Buzzy died in that manner, the poor horse must have starved to death. After all, many suggest, if he became lost in the snowstorm, he could have let the horse take him home. No one knows what took place that day, however.

Glowing objects in the dark of night, moving wherever she moved, must have been a nightmare for Mrs. Buzzy, and so the tale of the squid caper takes on new meaning. It is about the depths of life and death and what we are afraid of most.

Sunday, "Fun Time"

Newfoundland, as is the case with other provinces and countries, consists of many different religious sects. However, the largest numbers of people are Christian, so Sunday is primarily a day of togetherness and prayer at the church a family's of choice. Throughout the countryside, the youngsters would utter a collective sigh as if singing in the same choir, "Must I."

Uncle Jabe was a captain in the Salvation Army. Unfortunately, Uncle Jabe was hard of hearing. However, he was a fervent minister and loved to lead the singing of the congregation. One of his favorite hymns was *Down at the Cross*. The people liked it as well. The verse went, as I have heard it sung:

> It was down at the Cross
> Where I first saw the Light,
> And the burden of my heart rolled away.

> It was there by chance
> That I first saw the light,
> And now I am happy all the day.

I don't want to give the impression that my wife's family is composed disproportionately of hellions and rascals, but she tells this tale of her cousin who had gone to Uncle Jabe's Salvation Army service: when he sang the hymn, as loud as he could, the words were somewhat different than the rest of the congregation was singing:

It was down at the bar

Where I smoked my first cigar.

And the money in me pocket rolled
away.

It was there by chance

That I tore me Sunday pants,

And now I have to wear 'em every day.

Uncle Jabe would hear that exuberant sound and call out at the wonder of it. "That's right me son, sing out. Hallelujah and praise the Lord!" And the adults would hold their sides to keep from laughing while the other children laughed out loud and almost rolled in the aisles. Surely, Sunday services must have been well packed with parishioners who couldn't wait to see or hear what would happen next.

I Will Fear No Evil

Uncle John had discovered a sure way to avoid illnesses and disease, especially in church. It was his belief that he would be safe from all germs if he soaked his handkerchief in eucalyptus oil and waved it in the air around him. Also, every once in a while he would bring the cloth up to his nose to make sure that the air inhaled was safe as well. However, the people sitting within the immediate area were heard to mutter "yuck" at the odor emanating from Uncle John, and the congregation would move as far away from him in the pew as they possibly could without insulting the man. It mattered not to John, however, and he continued to incense the air.

I don't know why Uncle John never got ill. But never having to come face to face with another human just might have been the reason. Or just perhaps, God looked down kindly upon the old man and this eccentric habit and smiled.

A View from the Pew

In churches, however so quaint,

You'll always find some quirky saint,

One who's filled with religious ardor

And shows it as if he's in his parlor.

There are some who dread this fervent zeal,

Especially before the dinner meal.

They often look askance and frown

At those they think act like a clown.

Such acts as those are not really relevant,

Nor what those offended consider reverent.

Too bad they cannot share joy and love,

Which can only come from God above.

Love Thy Neighbor

The Americans have a harvest holiday that offers thanks to God for all the good bounty they have received during the year past. It is known simply as Thanksgiving. Historically, Newfoundland also had such a day of thanks, known simply as the Harvest Festival. Today, this holiday bears the same name as in the States. The Harvest Festival was under the aegis of the Church, which used tithing as a means of helping those less fortunate. If one grew a hundred pounds of potatoes, ten were brought to the church. No matter what the crop, ten percent was brought to the church. And the Newfoundlander gave of his own accord. Today he is still giving, but his donation is now in the form of exorbitant taxes. However, back in the good old days the average man was there to help others who needed help without the state interfering.

Uncle Ken, who lived around the Port Blandford area, was that kind of man, a person who helped others. He was truly God's man, with a good heart and love for others. He had his garden and his workshop, and he fished for food and hunted as well. He also had a young ward about the age of ten. During the hunting season this youngster would echo the same refrain every week. "Did you get your moose yet?" And every week the reply would be, "Not yet. I'll tell you when I do."

Finally, after a time had passed, the girl once again posed her query and the reply was positive, with the directive that it could now be told to all that Uncle Ken had gotten his moose. The area where Uncle Ken had his home was also home to many enfeebled persons, the victims of age, some other relatives and some unfortunate poor. It was remarkable that these people who could not get out hunting for themselves had a quarter of a moose to keep them through the long cold winter. But even more remarkable is the fact that Uncle Ken had shot the only sixteen legged moose in the world.

No Thanks Required

In the olden days, it was really rare

To go about hungry 'cause friends were there.

Veggies and fish and hunted meat

Were always provided for you to eat.

No one needed government largess.

The people donated as an act of kindness.

And although thanks was always readily given,

None was needed; they had their place in
heaven.

I must admit this still goes on today,

And that is why whenever I pray

I'm thankful for people in this human race

Who somehow manage to make this a better
place

Oh, the Newness of it All

Life as we know it today was different before people had the use of electricity. Electric lights brought about the demise of the kerosene lamp. Communication from one far off neighbor to another now is as simple as picking up the phone. Refrigeration meant that perishables could be protected from spoilage during the warm periods of the year. And it was during the introduction of this new electric age that new products made of new materials were mass produced for usage by the people in their homes and business. One of these products that we take for granted today was a new marvel for the turn of the century Newfoundlanders. Plastics, a new name and material, amazed the people because of its lightness, strength and versatility. Aunt Betty was an adventurous soul and she was one of the first to try it.

Aunt Betty bought dishes made out of plastic. One of the dishes was a container used to hold butter. In the cold winter and spring months Newfoundlanders didn't worry about preservation because food would freeze during the long cold nights within the house. When the rock hard butter had to be used, one would stoke up the wood fire and heat up the oven. They placed what they needed to heat in the oven and prepared to break the fast at the beginning of the day.

It was time to toast the bread and it was time to thaw the butter. As usual, Aunt Betty placed the plastic container of butter into the oven. A short time later she returned to check if the butter was thawed. Imagine her surprise when she saw that the butter had thawed, but the plastic container had melted as well.

This would never do! And as any housekeeper would, she took the melted container back to the store where she had bought it. She was not to be denied. Standing tall with her starched back and her eyes blazing, she demanded her money back. I don't know what the store manager said in return. But Aunt Betty still has that melted dish.

A Modern Convenience

When stories are related, they are told with a twinkle in the eye, a smile upon the lips and wistfulness for the old days. We take for granted the modern conveniences such as electricity and refrigerators that kept food fresh and cold. When electricity did come to the harbor town where my wife's aunt lived, her family soon bought a refrigerator because they had heard how easy it was to keep food for a long period of time.

In those days, getting an object like that was soon the talk of the town. Of course Aunt M liked to show it off to all the neighbors and relations. But soon there were problems. Aunt M would complain loud and long that the fridge wasn't any better than the cabinet she had used before.

"Now, what seems to be the problem?" asked the neighbor.

"The food don't last too long. In fact, my old cabinet was better," was the reply.

"Well, what's wrong with it?"

"Well, I puts in me food just as I did with me cabinet, and when I goes to sleep, I makes sure to unplugs the refrigerator to save electricity I wouldn't be using. When I wakes in the morning, I go to the box and opens the door, and sure enough the food is no good, and neither is that machine!"

Self Preservation

The coming of refrigerators was a boon to the local undertakers. However, the undertaker in one of the small towns in the area wore two hats. He served as the mortician, and in the case I know of, he was also the local grocer. These small stores sell everything that you can buy in your modern supermarket, but Mother would not buy meat in this particular market and extends her discrimination to all like markets to this day, whether a mortician ever ran it not.

She really was afraid the steaks, roasts, ribs and other meats would be stored next to a laid-out corpse. Her reasoning was that the body was sure to contaminate the food. If the corpse died of germs, the steak was sure to get it and pass it on. And if the person in question died of cancer, then you were assured of getting that as well. She felt that unless it was bovine, ovine, porcine, or chicken, then it shouldn't be in the market's freezer.

This fear is persistent and she will go to the next town to go to a gleaming supermarket or a meat market rather than buy locally. Most of her modern offspring laugh at her, but many of the old timers feel there's a lot of wisdom in her actions. Who knows?

The undertaker used the cold freezing temperatures that were only available in the winter. In the hot summer months, burial was immediate. But in the winter when the ground was rock-hard, the body could only be stored in the fish house on the strand. It wasn't unusual to see children make wide excursions around that location because they knew that Uncle Thomas was lying there. And when the night was upon the town and you were out late, you could feel the goose bumps build and knew the chill you felt was not the weather.

Creature Comforts

A life of ease is what I seek.

It makes life seem a little less bleak.

No more I have to stack the wood.

I flip a switch; the heat feels good.

No more the frozen chamber pot.

I get my relief in a nice warm spot.

Food lasts weeks without exaggeration,

In a modern kitchen with cold refrigeration.

Even in the inky dark of night.

I am blessed with electric light.

I sometimes sigh for the good old days

And even miss those hard old ways.

Perhaps, I'm getting lazy and soft.

But I don't sleep in a freezing loft.

I love creature comforts and what they bring

And I look to the future for any new thing.

House Beautiful

Imagine the most beautiful and grandest house in town. This is the kind of home that, when you walked by, you wished it was your own. This house was the show piece. It was well made. It was the best.

Unfortunately the old gentleman living out his years in his home finally succumbed when his time came and his name was called. As in most cases, the home was passed on to a relative, but what was she to do with this extra house? She did not want to leave her home, and the most expedient thing to do would be to sell. And sell she did.

A young couple, also related, bought the house years later. The day came to take possession, and after inserting the key and opening the door, they entered. They walked through each beautiful room, admiring what they saw, until they came to the master bedroom. There it was. The basin, the cloths and all the paraphernalia that was necessary to prepare the body for burial. They proceeded no further. They left the house never to return.

The young man was afraid of the haunting that would probably come to pass if they were to take up residence. Instead, he dismantled that house with its extra-wide wood planking, wood floors and plastered walls, but he would not even use the materials to build his own home upon the land.

Today, people still lament the tearing down of that house, and when I hear of

Historical Societies in the big cities that have to fight to save our heritage, I'm reminded of this tale. The shame is that the ghosts that reside within the minds of men are far more fearful than the spirits that have gone on.

That's Life

Why do we let superstition cause us strife

When there's no proof of unearthly life?

Why do we believe somebody's tales tall

When we know such things never happened at

all?

We never think like a realist,

But prefer the words of a fabulist.

And so we do such dreadful things

In the name of fate and what it brings.

How insecure we really feel,

If a weird tale makes us kick up our heels,

Causing us to hide and making us cower

Under the bedding covers in our cozy bower.

The cure for this is the realization

That we control the situation,

And we are the masters of our fate,

No matter the time and no matter the date.

The Starveling

Usually, in homes without electricity and therefore refrigerators, food was stored in pillowcases during the cold winter months. They were hung from the rafters in the bedroom to keep animals from raiding and stealing these provisions for the season. Because of the building costs involved, bedrooms usually did not have finished ceilings.

My friend Millie, when she was a young child, awoke in the middle of the night suffering from the pangs of hunger. She gazed wistfully at the pillowcase hanging from the rafters over her bed, then she turned and tried to go back to sleep. However, all she could think of was that sack tied above her head.

Throwing caution to the wind, she stood up on her bed, opened the pillowcase and discovered it contained a tube of that Newfoundland steak commonly known as baloney. This tube of baloney was wrapped in some sort of cloth and it was covered with wax to keep it preserved through the winter months.

Millie was stymied. What could she do? She looked about to see if there was some sort of cutting instrument that she could use open up that baloney in order to assuage her hunger. There was nothing to be seen. Millie was not to be daunted. Grabbing that tube and bringing it to her mouth, she began to gnaw at the wax. She spit out the hunks of wax into her hand and carefully hid them. Finally, she was able to tear into the cloth and arrive at her goal. She was in baloney heaven as she ate her fill of it. When she was done, she replaced the tube back into the case, tied it to the rafter and went blissfully back to sleep well sated.

Some time later in the season, Millie's mother retrieved the sack to prepare some boloney for dinner. She opened the sack and, taking out the tube, screamed and then shouted, "We've got rats in the house! They've eaten me baloney!" Millie's father came running into the room. He looked at the tube of baloney, and then he looked at the pillowcase, noting its pristine condition. He then looked directly at Millie and recounted, "I didn't know rats could untie pillowcases. Seems to me, what we got is two legged rats." Today, we think nothing of raiding the refrigerator, and it seems this idea existed in the old days as it does now.

We try to instill honesty in our children. Of course Millie wasn't dishonest, just hungry. Here was a member of the family who practiced a bit of thievery at a very young age, but I imagine all of us were tempted at one time or another, no matter how much instilling we received orally or on our backside. But my wife's mother would probably make modern psychologists cringe at the manner in which she handled the case of the missing ten dollar bill at grandma's house. Nevertheless, it has been proven that mother knows best.

Honesty: The Best Policy

Sister had to go on an errand to Grandma's house. As in most small towns, only throwing distance separated family homes, and so it was easy to send one of the youngsters when a relative needed help.

Grandma had a strange habit. Picture the windows framed with curtains that were tied back, causing a fold to extend out across the top half of the window. Now the kitchen table was placed in front of the window with three chairs surrounding it. Grandma would sit on the side of this table, and she had the habit of placing odds and ends into the fold of the curtain. There could be cards, letters and other sundry matters there, including money.

Mother had finished spinning wool. It was not dyed, and remained just the natural shades of sheep's color. Grabbing hold of sister, she dispatched her to Grandma's because she had asked for a skein to finish her knitting project. Sister, being the good child that she was, delivered the wool; and Grandma, being the sweet person that she was, invited her to have "lassy" bread and tea. She seated the child in her own special chair by that special tied-back curtain. She then turned to start the water boiling upon the stove and also to get the "lassy" bread.

Sister looked about the room as she had done a hundred times before, and then she looked at the edge of the curtain. And there it was. Only a corner of it showed, but she instantly recognized Newfoundland money, a ten-dollar bill. She didn't hesitate. She didn't think. But the money was in her pocket as she drank her tea and ate her "lassy" bread.

Later that day, mother had the occasion to go to the local store for some provisions. At the store, the proprietor asked how it was that sister had so much money to spend on candies and other goodies. Mother knew something was amiss. When she arrived home she confronted the culprit and discovered that the child had spent three of the ten dollars. Ten dollars at that time was a princely sum, and three dollars could have probably fed the whole family. Sister was in trouble. And mother's justice caused even more. She had spent three dollars, and for every dime contained in that amount she would have to work at Grandma's house for atonement.

There were thirty dimes spent, so there would be thirty hours of work at a rate of one hour each day for a month in retribution. Poor sister! Each day she would go to Grandma's house and wash and clean, wash and clean. And each day, when she looked at her reddened hands she knew how they got that way and what it meant to be dishonest. As I have said, "Mama knows best!"

Temptation

When you always have to pinch a cent

And wonder where your coins have went,

That's the time to fight temptation

And pray to God for your salvation.

So when easy lucre you espy,

Just leave it there and let it lie.

And the good you feel will make you glad

You didn't get whipped for being bad.

You'll walk about with head held proud

And people will nod and say aloud,

What a good one you really are,

And without a doubt you'll go far.

But there's a whim that's deep within,

And it really makes you want to sin.

You'll act just as a sneaky ferret,

While the crimes committed without a fret.

The time has come, alas alack.

It's a done deed, there's no turning back.

So try to enjoy those ill-gotten gains.

Try not to think of those rear-end pains.

Who will know what happened there?

The money vanished into the air.

You can buy whatever you like best,

And even manage to save the rest.

"I hear you Ma! What did you say?

I've been bad and I'll have to pay.

And I will suffer a time most long.

Oh, please forgive me for I've been wrong!"

But words will not suffice enough.

You'll have to show that you are tough.

For long and hard is the punishment,

So you'll not end up as a malcontent.

That Wonderful Newfoundland Rock

When the cold winters hit these coastal towns, isolating them with ice and closing them off from comforts we take for granted today, people learned to live with hardship and could even find fun with a frozen chamber pot. There were many who enjoyed making colored patterns on the frozen ice with their hot body fluids. I doubt if there is not any man or boy on any continent who has not used his pencil in such a fashion, be he writing on the frozen tundra or out upon the hot desert sands. Girls who played with dolls would cut a figure out of a catalog, along with the depicted dresses, and then licking the figure would freeze the dress to it. Yet in spite of the cold, their beds were warm because of the beach rocks that were heated in the oven, wrapped in towels and placed in the beds before retiring.

Picking the rock was a game that depended upon finding the right size, upon knowing the rock would not explode after being in the oven for a time. Today, we depend upon a geologist to find for us what the child of yesterday knew from experience.

The Old Beach Rock

It lies out there upon the beach,
Just within my grasping reach.
It seems to be of perfect size.
The kind that's sure to be a prize.

I'll take it home to my old dad,
Who I think will be really glad,
And he will carefully scrutinize
The rock I thought was such a prize.

He'll rub his fingers upon its surface,
And then he'll throw it in the fiery furnace.
We'll sit and look through the safety screens
To see if it blows to smithereens.

That rock will sit without any harm,

And I'll think of how it will keep me warm.

It'll be wrapped in towels under the blanket tight,

And I'll be cozy throughout the night.

Not for me, the icy bed,

With bedclothes pulled up over my head.

I'll sleep and dream all the more,

Thanks to that rock found on the shore.

Lost In Space

Another story about electricity, this one about the first radio, happened to Grandma. When the radio first came into existence, electricity was not always available to everyone. So electricity had to be generated in order to run these new fangled machines. This was done by the use of wind chargers, commonly called wind mills today, or by the use of a bicycle with some child peddling furiously. When Grandma got the radio, she turned it on and was enthralled by the music that was playing, but just before the song was finished, she reached over and turned the radio off. The others in the room asked in amazement, "Why did you do that?" She responded, "I want to save it so that Grandpa can hear it when he comes home."

A Grave Illumination

Electricity was slow in coming to the villages along the coast, and when it did, it was used sparingly. The village streets had no lighting, but they did place one lamp pole in the schoolyard and another in the churchyard. Now, the church cemetery was not far from town, just up the hill. When the lamp was lit at night, a strange light was seen from the cemetery, a light that did not appear to come from the light pole proper, and soon people would not come out at night. This was because they were afraid of the ghost that was evident by the light shining from the hillside graveyard. Days went by, and this strange light became the main topic of conversation in the homes of the town. People were convinced the town was haunted.

One young man, whom you've met in a prior story, was not to be daunted. He declared that he was going up that hill at midnight to rip that ghost to bits. That night, surrounded by his friends and half of the townsfolk, he began his slow ascent up the hill, carefully avoiding stepping on any of the gravesites. He was careful to keep a steady eye on the source of the light, and soon he arrived at the spot that emitted the eerie aura. And there, on the ground, at the base of a wooden cross, was an upturned paint can, the bottom nicely reflecting the light from one of the only two sources of light in the town. He lifted the can, and giving a great shout that the light was only a reflection, he proceeded back down the hill to the admiration of the crowd. And in that instant this local hellion became the local hero, though he suffered from all the slaps on the back and handshaking. Yet people still talk about the ghost in the graveyard, unconvinced by his discovery.

Apparition Appreciation

After the vale of tears,

If our loved one should appear,

Why should we have to fear?

Why shouldn't the living host

Treat the returning ghost

With the honor due one he loved the most?

Do you think the one who passed away

Would haunt you, as people say,

And make you dread each passing day?

There's no reason for superstition

And why we act in this foolish fashion.

It's caused by lack of an education.

For long ago we learned that this was so:

Those ghosts wreak havoc wherever they go.

So beware and watch, 'cause you never know.

I espouse a different thought,

That all the spirits really ought

To be loved for all past joys they brought.

So don't be afraid in the ebony night

And the eerie light that you might sight.

Remember, you loved them with all your
might.

Do You Remember

Newfoundlanders today are proud of their schools and the rich education that their children receive. However, it wasn't so long ago that the one-room schoolhouse existed. And prior to the Joey Smallwood regime, the confederation, teachers were not licensed. In the small villages of three hundred or so folk, the little ones were sent to schools sponsored by either the Church of England or the United Church. I use the term "sent" in a sardonic way, as the children walked to the schools no matter what the distance. No busses for them!

The schools were set up in rows, with the first row being the first grade and graduating upward to grade eleven. Reading, writing and arithmetic were the main thrusts of the curriculum, with a smattering of geography, history and some of the arts as could be added on. Of course, if you managed to finish the eleventh grade, you then could teach.

In those days, it was deemed more important that the child was a helper in the household than it was that he or she attends school. Confederation was good in that it brought qualified people to the system and a basic curriculum for all grades in all schools, and it made education mandatory.

For the most part, as was told to me, the children loved school. It offered a relief from the home environment, and above all it offered a window to the world. My wife can still recite passages and poems today that she learned by rote as a child. But that mental exercise has kept her sharp through the years. I'm also sure that my mother-in-law, who is well into her eighties and also just as bright, still considers these readings her own good fortune. But then they had no television to distract them, and radio was only available if the wind blew.

The close personal instruction that the students received on a one-to-one basis with young instructors with whom they could relate also helped create a meaningful and friendly educational experience. My wife loved school so much that on the weekends, during what would have been her play time, she would go down to the beach with her friends, to a huge rock with a flat side that served as her blackboard. And they would play "school." Who, today, would do such a thing? But oh how I wish they would. There are too many who can't wait to leave their schooling behind.

Life's Lesson

When I was young,

I had to learn

So I could earn

A life of ease.

And so I studied

Long and hard

To get money by the yard

And had no time for me.

And now I'm old

And long retired,

Having done the work required,

And all I do is rest.

So do as I say

And not as I did:

Earn your quid

When you've aged a bit.

Go have your fun

While you're still young,

Before climbing up that rung

For security and success.

For you will find,

When you've gotten older,

Regrets that you weren't often bolder

As the good times slipped away.

Buchans and the Pit

People on the peninsula talk about the great advancements that made life easier, such as electricity and indoor plumbing, that came about late in the last century. But they are amazed and find it hard to believe that a little town at the end of a long road in the central part of the island had these goodies in the latter part of the 1920s. Buchans, the birthplace of my wife, started as a junction and evolved into a mining town. The American Smelting And Research Company of the United States was instrumental in getting the mine going and upgrading the standard of life there. Refrigerators, heaters, radios, lights, movies, a skating rink, and most importantly, indoor plumbing were the norm when other areas of Newfoundland had none of these amenities.

Chamber pots became a thing of the past in Buchan, and the rough-hewn wooden hole in an outdoor shanty became extinct. The town was laid out as any typical borough, with main streets and crossing intersections. There were private separate homes and the row townhouses. Some of the private homes reflected the owner's social position, and today the home of the doctor from that era has become Buchans' museum.

Families had a chance to grow and flourish in this little town. Children had their schools and places to go where they could spend their time enjoying their young lives. Some of the play areas would be considered out of bounds by today's standards, however. There was a big ditch called the "big mucky." This ditch carried the water used to wash the ore away. The water was grey with the pollution it carried, and yet children ate of the blackberries that grew close to the banks of the ditch and are still alive to tell about it.

The men of Buchans were hard workers, and they belonged to a union, which was rare in those days I believe. They worked hard and played hard. As I hear it, they thought nothing of using igniter cord to blow up lunch boxes or to throw at one another as a rough form of humor. They liked a good fight, and lived life to the fullest as they could. But there was sadness as well. Too many went to work and never came home, leaving widows and orphans. This is what happened to Joe.

An Ode to Joe

There are numbered tags upon the wall,

Protected by glass

So that all who pass

Know.

A numbered tag was a man,

Once with life,

Family and wife.

Now gone!

There is a broad opening,

Water filled to the whole,

The Glory Hole.

A pit!

Look to the long ago past.

Trams down the road

With ore for a load.
Pay dirt!

The man descends by rope and ladder
To get to his station.
And work for his ration.
Alone!

There's abrasion upon the line,
A rending snap,
A falling in the trap.
Ending!

A body impaled upon an iron,
But there's a will.
To climb up that hill.
Returning!

The man returns to home and hearth,
The household's survival
Depending on his revival.
Death!

Now there's a numbered tag in a case,
Upon a wall
Down the hall.
Remember!

Passage

There are none who, although they may have compassion and love, can really speak to the loss felt by the death of a parent or friend, to the depths of that grief. But it is especially hard when a parent loses a child, the child you have watched grow and become a productive adult and then to feel the parents' pain of that awful waiting for that final day. No matter where in the world we are, as humans, we keen and mourn such a terrible loss. But there is an answer. The answer is faith. Although I am no expert, I would suspect that the greater number of religions believe that life goes on beyond our scope. One of my Newfoundland friends who has become like a brother to me has suffered such a loss. This poem is for him and to ease the passage of his beautiful daughter, Sheilagh.

Renewal

Deep within the mind and body of my being
>I know that a small part of me,
>A bit of the spirit of me,
>Will in time return to the natal Godhead
>of us all.

This place, this earth, and this home I have,
>For me and mine is nothing
>But the womb for the passage
>Of this spirit, this bit of me to God.

No longer will the troubled bindings and ills
>Deter this rebirth to that love
>That gives meaning to life,
>That loves us all.

But ah, the black doubts that besiege me

    Bring sorrows at the thought

    Of death and separation,

    And I grieve in dark despair.

Thus I must have the faith and believe

    In that renewal, the newness

    And the different life

    We will all be born into.

And deep within the mind and body of my
being,

    I really know that a small part of me,

    A bit of the spirit of me

    Is with me always here and after.

Billy Buck

There was a time in those coastal towns on the Avalon Peninsula when it was more expedient to let the livestock run freely through the town. It was not unusual to see the "billy buck," the male goat, let loose amongst the ewes to do what has to be done to ensure that there are more animals in the future. Our graveyard hero had the only ram in town, and the goat had been roaming free for quite some time and developing an attitude.

The winter months were approaching, and the billy buck was soon rounded up to be put to work pulling a sled or doing any other task that required its strength. My new brother-by-law took that old goat up into the woods to bring back a small supply of fire wood. He hitched the goat to the sled and commanded the animal to move, but the billy buck gave him a look and stood his ground. "Bro" tried everything to make that goat move. He shouted, pleaded, pulled on him and even gave him a whack. Nothing would make old billy budge. "The heck with you, then," my in-law cursed. And he tied the goat to the tree, thinking he would come back later when the goat had seen the error of his ways.

Arriving home, he stoked the fire and settled down in his chair. He had worked hard all day, and the episode with the goat had gotten on his nerves. He was tired, and soon he was asleep and snoring. He awoke the next morning and discovered upon looking out the window that a foot of snow had fallen that night. Throwing on his coat, he rushed out the door and climbed up the slope to where that poor animal was still tied to the tree and looking like a snow sculpture of a goat. "Lard Jesus," my in-law muttered, "I hope that billy is still alive." To his great relief the goat was breathing, and he claims that you could almost feel the joy emanating from it at seeing his benefactor. Joe quickly untied the goat, and in an instant that goat was pulling the load. And as the story goes, my new relation never again had any trouble making that goat do whatever he wanted. I think there is a moral somewhere in this story.

Togetherness

Man and beast are never far apart.

They work together; it's from the heart.

But every now and then a thought

Makes man or beast do what's naught.

And without malice they upset each other

And make one another think they are a bother.

Each will punish the miscreant's crime,

If not now, then at a later time.

And after which there's repentance

And sorrow for their comeuppance,

And each will wait to try again

And never think about the pain.

The Good Book tells of the supremacy of man,

But it's the beast of burden that can

Bear the load and haul it too,

And make life easier for me and you.

Near Miss

Today, Newfoundland is still blessed with animals roaming freely. I have spotted moose during my yearly drive on the Trans Canada Highway from Port Aux Basque to Saint Johns. I know enough to watch carefully for wildlife and the other drivers simultaneously, because once I almost slammed into a car in front of me because the driver was thus distracted.

The driver had been traveling west on the TCH, not too far from Saint Johns, when she came to a sudden stop because, on the opposite side of the road, stood a large moose with a big antler spread. She jumped out of the car with her camera and proceeded to cross the highway to get a photograph. Fortunately, the vehicles behind me were a good distance away and were able to adjust to the situation by slowing down as I did and proceeding around the foolish person who stopped without pulling off the road. But others have had accidents involving not only with other cars but head-on collisions with moose. This is an increasing problem, and warning drivers is not enough. With the herd as large as it is, perhaps some of the stringent rules for the selection of hunters could be eased. But why make it easier to feed one's family?

I have come up on herds of elk on the southern coast that welcomed my car as a long lost brother. And of course there are always the idiotic rabbits who commit suicide daily. Newfoundland is also blessed with countless types of birds, and as beautiful as they are, I resent they're making my car their particular target.

Idiom

On some road somewhere in Newfoundland there is work being done, which is readily understandable because of the stresses of weather, cars and trucks. Drainage is a priority, and most of the work being done is in regard to this prime concern. The excavators that are used are of a size and look that can only make you think of dinosaurs of a bygone age. Unfortunately, my car had the experience of meeting one and trying to get to know it on a personal basis.

The warnings the authorities and the construction companies provide are excellent, which allows you to know what lies ahead well in advance. And so you are prepared to slow down and follow what the sign person tells you to do. And on this occasion I did. I stopped when I was told to stop and I proceeded when I was told to go. So I inched my car alongside of this giant behemoth when it swung its back end into the side of my car. I was stunned. The machine stopped its momentum and I was able to pull up and out of the way.

My wife is an expatriate of Newfoundland and she immediately took charge of the situation. Don't let a foreigner do the talking is the general rule of thumb. She said, "Wait for the Mounties," and we did. As we waited, she went about getting as much information as she could and getting a consensus that we were certainly not at fault. But I remember one truism uttered by one of the workers that seems universal for most people in most countries.

He, in all seriousness, coined an adage that all who don't want to get involved should always say to anybody in authority. It went like this, "I didn't see anything, and if I did see anything, I still seen nothing."

Grassroots

Why is it that we, being the animals that we are, seem to band together well enough but can't live without making all sorts of regulations to help us lead better lives than what we had going for us when we started? It seems that as life progressed and Newfoundland grew, a new group was created from hot air and bluster, and these became known as politicians. Now there came a time when a choice had to be made. The choice was whether to maintain the status quo, confederate with Canada or to have economic union with the United States. It was at this time in her life that my wife had a chance to be a star.

This was a period in her life when her mother had suffered hard economic times, partly caused by the death of her husband at the mines and also because of the number of children she had to rear. She asked her sister if she would help by taking a child to care for a period of time. My wife's mother's sister agreed, and soon my wife was ensconced in another house far from her home by the bay.

Now Auntie was a staunch conservative and a religious woman. She did not like Mr. Smallwood and his political policies and ideals. My wife, her aunt and daughter lived in a very small town where everyone knew each other. They all lived along the side of a straight road, with the track for the Newfoundland Bullet on the other side of the road, and other local homes on the other side of the tracks. Auntie's house was somewhat up the hill, with a lawn sloping down to the road. At the edge of the road and the lawn and marking the beginning of the drive was a big rock where my wife would sit and play as a child.

It was Election Day, and Auntie placed this innocent child upon that big rock at the juncture of the driveway and the road. She then admonished the child to sing at the top of her voice. She sang this song to the tune of "A Mother's Love is a Blessing." She had to sing this as the people in the town passed by on their way to vote. She did this for many, many hours. For being such a good girl, she received all the cookies she could eat and red syrup to drink in compensation. I can't imagine how sick she got on those treats and libation, and she claims she can't remember. I'm inclined to think she doesn't want to. This is what she sang:

Don't vote confederation,
And that's my prayer to you.
We own the house we live in,
Likewise the dory too.

But if you vote Joe Smallwood,
And his line of French patois,
You'll be always paying taxes to
The men in Ottawa.

It is interesting to note that Mr. Smallwood lost on the first count.

Riding the Rails

The Newfoundland Bullet is a part of the lore of the small towns. People point with pride to where the old tracks lie. They still speak of relatives who worked on her and how at one time they rode that line.

The one bit of information I gleaned was that once the train actually stopped at a trestle for twenty-four hours, and no one thought this to be unusual or complained. They simply made do. However, the train made a reputation that is carried fondly in the hearts of many old timers who wish that it were running today.

The Newfoundland Bullet

On a one-track road that ran both ways,

Passing by the ice cold bays,

Ran the Newfoundland Bullet from East to West

At a speed that was far from being the best.

And as you traveled far from end to end,

I hope you had a very good friend

To talk and laugh and pass the time

Or to play card games for a nickel and dime.

You ride with head pressed against the pane,

And it never helps if you complain.

And if you end up with some neuralgia,

Remember its part of the old nostalgia.

I have heard it said, they traded the track

For a Canadian road that runs there and back.

No more the steam and the lonely whistle,

You hear only trucks passing by the trestle.

And as I ride my quad along that way,

I wish they had let the old Bullet stay.

The fun is gone, now it is just a long car ride.

The bullet's gone into history along the
wayside.

Survival

In our time medicine has advanced in all areas and today our first thought when we need a doctor is to find one and to go to his or her office.

This was not always the case, especially if you lived and worked far from a hospital or a doctor.

My wife broke her arm at a young age. She went crying to her Uncle, who in his wisdom called his brother. Without hesitation, while one brother pulled and straightened the arm, the other held tight to the bawling child. Using kindling wood to make splints, they tied the arm and she held the splinted arm close to her side for a period until the bone was set and she no longer felt any pain. The arm and elbow were stiff after the splints were removed. However, the innate common sense and wisdom of these coastal pioneers provided the physical therapy to make the arm not only whole but flexible as well. For the next several weeks, wherever she went, she had to hold a sad iron in her grasp and constantly bend the arm up and down. Today, her bicep is greater in strength than mine is and I dare not challenge her.

Dentistry was another problem, and I know of too many instances when teeth have been pulled without the benefit of painkillers. Newfoundlanders were and still are the hardiest of people.

These practices no longer exist because you can now get to a hospital within an hour in most parts of the country. Yet I know of one town on the southern coast that refused resettlement, and it depends upon the availability of a helicopter to provide fast transportation to receive medical attention. Some things never change.

This town has no paved roads and entry to it is by a ferry that is owned and operated by the town. The town has its own schools and hydroelectric plant, and everything that is needed is ferried across the bay. The beauty of the place is that buildings are still being erected and people still come to settle in a village of peace and tranquility.

The main occupation is fishing, which is still practiced despite the restrictions. The small harbor is filled with dories and long liners. However, there was a time when some of the endeavors of the locals were not so licit. On the strand is a house that stands out from all the others. I do not know whether it stands out because it is a two-story or because of its proximity to the beach, but the house is striking and it draws you to it. Why? I can't explain, but I approached it with trepidation. But I had not to worry as two hardy fishermen invited me in and we got into a grand discussion of the times, fishing and some of the history of the house. It seems that at one time the house was not empty as it is now. It housed people and sheltered them from the weather and other folk. Today, however, it is filled with fishing gear such as netting and lobster pots. But back in time, even during its empty years, there were much goings on.

Fishing obviously depends upon nature. She dictates the time to harvest the lobster and the crab, the time to net the shrimp, and the time to fish for the cod, salmon and other finny creatures, and also the famous squid jigging time. Today, however, it is no longer legal to jig for squid. In the past, it was after many of these successful runs that the men would gather together to tie one on. Or for that matter, if any moment was right, what better to do than to have a party.

As if by magic, the old house would come alive, and amidst the sounds of laughter would be heard the clink of the glass and the clunk of the bottle as it was set down. This would continue through the night, only to be repeated many times in later days.

To this day I do not know where all those bottles came from, and I know better than to ask. But the most amazing thing I encountered in that old house, as the fishermen showed me through the rooms, is that I know I heard the clink and the clunk as I walked on through. I believe that, if ever anyone goes there with a beer in his belly and a light heart, he too will hear the clink and the clunk.

The Ren Contre East Phenomenon

The church is gone.

The houses are too.

The men, women and children,

They too are gone from view.

Only the ghostly crosses

Remain there to be seen

To remind the rest of us

What was and might have been.

Where have they gone?

What caused this devilment?

The answer my friend

Was resettlement!

So gone are the people,
The neighbors and friends,
Gone far from these shores
For political ends.

Yet the rebuke is there
In that town by the sea,
And Ren Contre East remains
As it used to be.

No government shackles
Upon their lives and ways.
They live as they used to,
In the good old golden days.

They are the spirits
Of the united Newfoundlandian,
Who feel their independence
Will end up in oblivion.

Thus their quaint response,

To every query's bit,

Is, "Living in Isolation,

And loving it!"

Investiture

Squid jigging time has been told about in stories and written of in song. I know of a man who came to this wondrous island when squid jigging was still allowed. He was a man from the states, and his clothing was different from the garb worn by the natives. He often wore white shirts and slacks, and because his in-laws were fisher folk, they invited him to go out in the harbor and jig for squid. What a time that would be, he imagined. A time to sit in the boat upon the quiet water and a time to drink a beer and a time to talk, laugh and relax.

The boat was pushed off from the shore. The motor soon roared into life, and the boat headed for its watery destination. When they reached the grounds, they anchored and gave the neophyte definite and particular instructions. "Now here's whatcha have to do. After you drop the jig, you kinda bounce it off the bottom. You can feel when you get squid on the line. Haul 'er in and be sure when you get the squid off the jig you hold 'er high over your head so that it don't slip out and fall back into the water."

"Okay. I got the idea," he told them.

The men sat and jigged, talked of various things and finally, as luck would have it, my friend managed to hook as many squid as his jig could hold. "I got 'em!" he shouted, all excited at the prospect of getting his first load of squid.

"Remember now, hold that squid high over your head."

"I know. I know."

So he hauled on the load and pulled in the line. Grasping the jig loaded with squid, he held it high over his head.

The others in the boat roared with laughter. They held their bellies because of the pain caused by the laughter. They pointed their fingers at him and soon pulled out rags and towels.

Newfoundlanders love a prank and a chance to get one better on anybody. Here he was, this man in his jacket, white shirt and slacks, a man who knew nothing about squid but wanted to be part of the crew, to be considered one of them, and they bamboozled him. What they neglected to tell him in their particular instructions is that the squid would defecate and spill its ink when it was out of the water.

There he sat, this man from the States in his fecal jacket looking chagrined and feeling foolish, but he was definitely laughing with them. As for his jacket, his poor wife had the chore of cleaning up the mess. However, he kept his hat unkempt and unclean as a reminder and also as a trophy.

There was a Time

There was a time not so long ago

When the dories were strung out row on row,

And they crossed the harbors 'til out of sight,

And the people fished from dawn 'til night.

But now all is different and the fishing is
rough.

They've closed the harbors and things are
tough.

No more the salted flakes upon the shore.

The boats aren't out there any more.

No more the bloody scenes of piscine gore.

You buy nice clean fish at the country store.

And the families raised by this noble
occupation,

Rely instead upon governmental compensation.

Only if you're in the licensed class

Can you fill your boat as the seasons pass.

And the cry for justice falls on deafened ears,

And the poor stay poor throughout the years.

Caplin Time

Mother Nature's generosity in regards to fishing is legendary. My wife still talks about the size of cod that were caught and the vast numbers there were for the taking. We, as custodians, have not been very good to "Mom." We have raked the bottoms clean, and even more troubling, we have hindered the natural reproductive environment. One of the species of fish the old timers depended upon, because they realized how important this concept of custodianship was, is a smelt-like fish called caplin. This wondrous fish was used not only for food but also for fertilizer. Many of the beautiful trees, flowers and vegetables owe their growth to the caplin.

The female of the species would come into the shore to deposit her eggs, and the male followed in order to complete the reproductive cycle. This "rolling" would take place for several days, usually at night in the summer, and the neighboring towns would anxiously await the arrival of the fish every year. People would telephone up and down the shore asking if the caplin had come in. There was much excitement for the village people, waiting and watching for the rolling. When it happened, people would scoop them up by the bucket full. Over and over they would roll, and over and over the people scooped, but the caplin was never wasted. And most importantly, the caplin was the harbinger of good news. For following the caplin were the cod, which fed upon them, and whales and other types of fish also. However, the caplin harvest has grown less and less in recent years, and the cod are taken in smaller numbers as well.

The native Newfoundlander has suffered under a moratorium that has lasted years. Only the professional can go out in his long liner and fish the cod to any great extent. The native is limited to a grand total of thirty cod, which have to be tagged and can only be caught at a certain time of the year. I'm sure the government knows when the cod are coming. Certainly, the caplin know and so does the average native fisherman.

'Tis the Time

Waiting, waiting, waiting,

There's expectation in the air,

And the people ever asking,

Neighbors, kin and friends, "Where?"

Walk the shorelines,

And watch the flying gulls.

Catch the glimmer on the water,

Hear the slap upon the hulls.

Coming, coming, coming,

See black streaks upon the sea,

And the silent witness points

To what is yet to be.

Cold and cool and clammy
Is repeated year by year,
And the people know what's coming
For the caplin time is here.

Hustle, hustle, hustle,
Grab the bucket, pail or pot,
And gather up the harvest,
Good fortune is our lot.

And the silent witness upon the beach
Foretells another omen,
And the people laugh with joy,
Because the cod is comin'.

I Got Me Rights

Everybody has, or at least some of us have, a crazy aunt or an uncle. I'm not completely sure about what happened when or the time line, but this is a story about my crazy uncle by way of marriage.

Uncle Herb lived in the town of Catalina, which is in the central portion of Newfoundland, on the road to Trinity. He was a simple man who did his chores, did some hunting and often enough fishing. He was not a wasteful man but simply took what he needed to survive. He also was a religious man, and to coin a phrase, he believed in Devine Right. And then it happened: the moratorium! No more free access to fishing. No more of the cod or the lobster to stave off hunger. This moratorium did not stop Uncle Herb, however.

He continued to fish, but after some time, the game warden found out about it and visited Uncle Herb. "Now you mustn't be fishin' or goin' after lobster, Herb," warned the game warden. "It is the law now, and everybody has gots to follow the rules."

"Oh yes I am goin' fishin'. The good Lord made the ocean with all the fish in it and he made man to eat the fish, and I am goin' to do that," was Uncle's answer.

"Well, I'm warning you, and if I catch you at it again, I'll take your load and fine you too."

"You can fine me all you wants, but I'm goin' fishing and you're not gettin' me fish. The good Lord put that lobster there for me to eat, and you won't stop me from doin' the Lord's work."

With that both men stalked off, each going in a different direction.

The next time out, a few days later, Uncle was caught again by the warden, and as promised, the warden fined him and took the fish. However, the warden had one last word. "The next time I'll be arrestin' you if I catches you at it again."

A small threat such as jail time didn't daunt this stalwart man, however. He proceeded to fish once again, and once again the warden caught him and had him arrested. I don't know if the judge sent him to jail or let him go, but I do know this, there was a next time.

The season was getting on, and Uncle Herb was going to go birding. So he had his shotgun as well as his fishing rod with him in the boat. Sure enough, he had no sooner gotten out on the water when the warden appeared in his boat and waved Uncle to the shore. Try to imagine the scene. Both men were probably fuming. The warden felt that this authority was being ignored, and Uncle surely felt the warden had gone too far. They got out of their boats upon the rocky shore and the warden approached Herb shouting, "When are you going to do what you're supposed to do?"

"If I tolds you once I tolds you a thousand times, I ain't ever goin' to stop doin' what the Lord provided me to do. Now stop tormentin' me and get out of me way."

And with that Uncle took his shotgun out, raised it and blew a monstrous hole in the game warden's boat.

"Are you crazy?" screamed the warden!

Uncle simply waved the gun and the warden was last seen running as fast as he could and as far as he could away from Uncle.

I do not know what happened after that. I wasn't there. I can only report that the judge was heard to say, "That man's crazy. Its best we leave him alone." And they left him alone for the rest of his life. He may have been crazy

as they say; I feel he's as crazy as a fox.

Out to Dinner

Not everyone defied the moratorium and got away with it. Some said, "The heck with it!" and went out and fished as if nothing had changed, and this is what happened to some people I've been told about.

It was a great day to go out into the harbor. The sun was out; the ocean was calm and the temperature just right. And so they did. They pulled in the boat from its mooring, piled in and set out for the secret spot they knew would hold cod ready to snap at the lures upon their lines. And they fished. The time passed, and when they had enough, they hauled the anchor and set out to return home. They secured the boat at the mooring again, and they cleaned the fish, which made the gulls and crabs happy. The only thing left to do was to build a fire on the beach, fry up some fish and enjoy the end of the day.

What a wonderful meal. Nothing surpasses fresh cod, good company, and good conversation. But they were interrupted when a stranger approached. "Come join us for a bite to eat," they called out. "Don't mind if I do," was the reply. So he sat and joined in the good times. Too soon the time came when the repast was finished and they had to leave. At this point, the new friend, the stranger, stood up, produced his credentials and proclaimed he was the fish warden. He then confiscated the rest of the catch and gave them a citation.

They paid their fine, and as I have heard, it amounted to the large sum of five hundred dollars. It turned out to be the most expensive fish dinner they ever had. But I've also heard it was not their last.

Whatever It Takes

There is a fine line between superstition and religion. Often we share both attributes at the same time, with greater credence given to either superstition or religion given the situation at hand. I had to find a friend within the Irish Loop whose exact address I did not know. It was easy to find the house when I arrived at the town, because everybody knows everybody in the small towns of Newfoundland, and when I asked, the information was easily attained.

I found the house and went to the side door. I knocked, rang the bell and shouted. Nobody was home. I did not even try the front door, as many of the houses are built with mother-in-law doors. That is, there is a door but no steps leading up to it. You can guess why that particular door is called by this name. Nevertheless, I was curious and walked out to the back where a shed was located. I had a vague thought that possibly my friend might be working in that small building. I went in, looked around and spotted what seemed to me an oddity. There were folded slickers upon the work bench, and laying on that pile was an oiled hat with a strand of rosary beads coiled neatly around the brim. I had just picked up the hat and was studying t closely when I heard the truck arrive, and still holding the hat I went out to meet my buddy.

"Hi, when did you get here?" he said as he gave me a bear-like hug.

"Just a moment ago. I knocked, rang the bell and shouted, but there was no answer. So I looked in the shed, thinking you were there, and found this."

"That's my father's hat. He used that when he went out fishing."

"I realize that. What is strange to me is the fact that it has these rosary beads wrapped around it."

"And why not? He just wanted to make sure he returned safe."

You figure it out. Which part of this is superstition and how much of it is religion?

Soul Food

The appeal of religion is strong to the hardy folks who inhabit the Rock; but many of the sects have various taboos, and your entry into heaven will be ensured if only you follow the true faith and do not violate those taboos. Aunt Bidey was a believer in such things.

The early times produced families that were dependent upon the land. They maintained a vegetable garden. They tended the animals. They hunted and fished for provisions, and in general, they were self sufficient. Uncle Ken would raise a pig and slaughter it when the time came to get the family through the winter, but his aunt believed pork was the "devil's food." She followed that Hebraic tenet of not eating animals with cloven feet and the inability to chew their cud.

So, if Ken's children visited, she would invariably fill their ears with her stern adage: "You're not eatin' that old dirty pork, are you?" Of course, after a period of time, this began to stick in their craw. There was only one solution. Tell Uncle Ken. And being the practical man that he was, he had the ideal reply.

The children went back to Aunt Bidey, and she began her usual tirade. They, however, were ready. "Uncle Ken told us, 'What goes in the body will never hurt the soul.'" Aunt Bidey was infuriated, and she was stubborn too. She ignored the statement and held to her belief that pork was a forbidden meat. And no matter how many times the children came to visit, the same script was played over and over again.

Never doubt the power of religion or superstition.

Forbidden Fruit

Some say there are taboos decreed by God,
And I really find that awfully odd.
I think when Eden first was made,
There were fish in the sea and animals in the glade.

And in the Good Book it was understood,
That for Eve and Adam life was good.
Life went on without a sin,
But curiosity did them in.

So now we play the part of God
And make up taboos most frightfully odd.
And for our sins recompense,
We've given up our common sense.

Beware the Pixies upon the Land

Do not think, however, that superstition was not a definite part of life in the "old" days. Fairies were to be feared. When my mother-in-law sent her children out to pick blueberries, she would make the children wear some article of clothing inside out because she believed that the fairies would not take you away if you did. Today, it you were to go to the Brigus Blueberry Festival and take the walking tour of that wonderful old town, you would witness a small skit attempting to show what could happen to you if the fairies got you. It looks and sounds much like *A Midsummer Night's Dream*, but the point is well made.

Summer Pickings

On gravelly, rocky hill sides

Or boggy, scrubby barrens,

In midst of somewhat desolation,

At midsummer

There is life!

Cars will park all about,

And the area,

If seen from high above,

Through the wispy clouds,

Is like an ant farm.

There the hum and buzz of people

And the quiet thud of plastic pails,

Cans and containers

Held by the gnarled fingers

That pick the blue treasure trove.

Pushing aside leaves
To reach each globule ready to burst,
Its blue stain on hands, mouth and teeth,
While the orbs are piled high
To be recreated.

Sold on country roads or in grocery stores,
To homes with secret recipes
For all the goodies
Of cakes, pies, ice cream and wine
To be enjoyed.

And parties, festivals, galas and fetes
Are held to give homage and honor
To that fabled fruit
The Newfoundlander loves to eat:
The blueberry.

Blessings

The most meaningful story, superstition, religious tale, or what have you involves a time called, Old Christmas Day. This is a day when no one will go into the barn, because it is said that on this day you will find all the animals on their knees praying. I would readily join them, but I'm afraid that I would not be considered good enough.

The Replacement

Today the "quad" or "trike," an all terrain vehicle, is the workhorse for the man who labors to keep his home warm by stacking enough wood to last him through the winter. As wonderful as this machine is, it was to be the downfall of a unique and wonderful animal known as the Newfoundland pony. In the past, the pony served as the beast of burden, hauling the wood, helped with the plowing, and it was the engine of transportation.

Unlike other horses, the pony evolved into a breed that could stand the warm summers and suffer the cold winters without ill effects. It was an easy animal to care for and nurture. It was also one of a kind. In many households it might have been considered one of the family. There were approximately three to four thousand horses at work on the island during the peak years of its use. So what has happened that today there are only about one hundred and fifty left?

I can remember during the Second World War, when beef was hard to get, that we as a nation (the United States) chose to imitate the French and eat horse meat. My parents and I ate it primarily for sustenance and never developed a taste for it. Unfortunately, the French liked it too much and the Japanese savored the taste as well. When the ATVs started being used, there was no need to keep the horses and an industry started. Meat wagons, trucks, would visit the various homes that harbored the pony, buy them and deliver them to the slaughter houses to be butchered.

The meat was then exported to the French and the Japanese. Some was possibly made into dog food.

The pony's plight was soon recognized by the noted Newfoundland artist, Cliff George, and groups such as the Newfoundland Pony Society and Newfoundland Pony Care Inc. They would follow the route of the slaughter trucks and try to buy the horses before the trucks got to the horses' owners. Today, there are sanctuaries run by these groups where the horses are cared for and run free.

I tell you this to show that, despite their penchant for pranks, the Newfoundlander also has a good heart filled with compassion and love.

The Newfoundland Pony

The Newfoundland Pony,

He's short of leg with a shaggy mane.

He can stand the hot summer heat

And the cold winter strain.

He's always ready to do the work,

And he's always near at hand.

There's no other pony like him,

And he's found only in Newfoundland.

But progress was his downfall.

He's been replaced by automation.

And they paid him for his service

With partial annihilation.

He's become fodder for the masses;

He's become a source of food.

And all the foreigners loved him
Because he tasted really good.

But other Newfoundlanders cared
About the pony's plight.
So they set out to save the horses,
And they tried to make things right.

And today the herd is growing,
And they still do work for men,
But now the owners love them,
And for that I say amen.

Ageless City

During the war years, I never got the chance to be stationed in St. Johns and so was not one of those responsible for the exodus of many of the wonderful and beautiful women by marriage to the soldiers of the US. But St. Johns offered an escape for the rural lass and a chance for betterment of living conditions, work, and the fulfillment of dreams. There were parks, museums, restaurants, dances, events and a myriad of things to do and see. I wish I had been there.

This Newfoundland city can rival cities anywhere in the world, perhaps not in size but for the wonderful exuberance of life and living found there. St. Johns is the oldest city on the North American continent. Shipping and aqua business probably constitute the primary sources of wealth, but it is also home to artists of all types and the Capital as well. There are certain streets that develop an aura that attracts people from all over the world to see. Such is the heartbeat of St. Johns.

The Heartbeat of St. Johns.

Rag tag scamps of uncertain ages

Parade the streets of Saint Johns.

Wiser than the city sages,

They twist and dodge around the town.

There are some of varied tinted hairs

Who sit slopped over with incessant chatter

In battered matching painted wooden chairs,

While others evade the places they gather.

The special streets with their special stores

Lure the shuffling feet to enter in,

And they, losing inhibitions galore,

Find liquid absolution for their sins.

The ogling eyes seek each other out,

And trysts are arranged for the ensuing night

Amid the touch and sweat that brings about
Bodies welded hot, wet and tight.

Brassy sounds producing wails
Or chants of Irish songs
Bring emotions to the fore
And thrill the happy throngs.

The music, noise and wild gyrations
Go unabated in the endless tempo,
And the weary watch with fascination
As vulpine revelers dance fast and slow.

Though the cockerel no longer is there to crow,
The early dawn arrives cool and sweet,
And the worn bodies trudging down the row
Leave Duckworth, Water and old George
Street.

While round these limits people watch and
smirk,

With snobbish noses high in the air,

At those who the ancient normalcy they shirk

And close their eyes to what's happening there.

So life goes on in this great city,

With all the colors and in all the places,

And strangers come to share the joy

Of old St. Johns' amazing graces.

Initiation

Today, it is a conglomeration of many of the old and new factors that make up the Newfoundland culture. Most natives know that the rum named Screech was called that because after taking one sip that is what you did, for example, but tourism has also become an important industry. And to entertain the tourists, many families do a "Screeching In," which is said to create honorary Newfoundlanders. This cheapens the true love that many strangers feel for the island. However, the ceremony does create a feeling of belonging and of being one with the land and with the people.

My mother-in-law is well into her eighties. Yet she still goes to all the parties, dances and generally has a good time. If challenged, she will easily bend over and touch her toes to show how agile she is. Old age won't claim her either physically or mentally, and she still looks to the future by constantly buying lottery tickets. She knows that someday she is going to hit the big jackpot. She also claims that she has fished in all the ponds between Trinity Bay and the city of St. Johns. Her addiction to fishing goes beyond understanding, and it was during a "Screech In" held by her grandchildren and in-laws that she proved just how bad her affliction is.

The victims were seated upon a make-shift throne with their bare feet ensconced in a tub containing all manner of objects in the murky water. They were dressed in slickers and oils, draped with the flag of Newfoundland

and listening to the gibberish of the officiating crew. They repeated as they were told, ate what they had to eat, and drank what they had to drink. And most importantly they kissed what they had to kiss.

These were my mother-in-law's in-laws, friends and her grandchildren participating in a ritual they neither understood nor really wanted to experience, but for the fact that their participation would make entertainment for the family and possibly themselves. Later they would get their certificates making them honorary Newfoundlanders, and this fact, more than the ceremony, would make them feel proud that they were really so, at least for that moment. This woman stayed in place all of five minutes and then quietly edged to the rim of the crowd so she could sneak down to the pond where her fishing pole lay. As others watched that awful rite, she cast out her line upon the waters. The other fishermen standing on the bank had been there for a period of time, but with her skill and knowledge she had caught three fish by the time the relatives realized she was missing and went to the shore to retrieve her. I know people who had an easier time giving up cigarettes than she could give up that sport. And besides, those trout were good eating!

At Mom's oldest daughter's fiftieth wedding anniversary, the politicians stood at the dais to give honors to the couple. I will never forget the honorable who said that, of all the many occasions honoring fifty years of marriage in which he had participated, this was

the first time the mother of the bride was there.
God bless her.

My Fishing Mama

Of all the fish I've ever eaten,

The best were those caught by cheatin'.

Be it cod or any other,

I love the ones that were caught by Mother.

She fished them here; she's fished them there;

She said she's fished them everywhere.

Along each rocky pond or lake,

The trout were there for her to take.

Whether in season or whether not,

Bake them, fry them and serve them hot.

But you must know I'm being bold,

So don't believe what you've been told!

We all follow what our leaders say,

And never ever go astray,

But if you're like all the rest,

Remember Mama knows what's best!

The Trouble Maker

Newfoundlanders love a party. It is another chance for fun and excitement. It is a release from the hard work and the gray skies that can affect your outlook on life. And it doesn't take much to get a party started. Finding the house of a friend or relative is the first step, and the rest comes easy.

We went to visit my sister-in-law, and soon a neighbor came and stayed for a little "Screech" and coke. Not long after, one of the other in-laws arrived, and then some other friends. The freezer was opened, and bundles of food were taken out and slightly nuked in the microwave. The hamburgers, hot dogs and various fish were soon on the bar-be-cue under the supervision of "Bro".

Loads of fun! The drinks helped to unloosen inhibitions, which led to singing, good conversation and festivities. One in particular I remember was the placing of imitation tattoos on particular parts of the anatomy. How the women convinced the men to put them on the upper areas of their rumps is mind boggling. As I was one of the participants, I can only marvel at it. Unfortunately, there are pictures to prove I did it. No protests from me.

And so the time went, and soon farewells were made and we all went back to our various abodes to sleep well and to vow that we would get even by having a party of our own to share.

I've spoken before about the caginess of the natives of this northern clime. I've shown the love of a prank that often can be hurtful. This particular party was a big success. It started as a small visitation and ballooned into soiree, but not all our friends knew about it and not all our relatives.

I would guess that small feuds occur in most families from time to time, and they can be short-lived. However, it only takes one to make sure the battle is extended. Such is what happened after the Gathering. There is a person who is on the outs with one side of the family. There is another person who wished to stir up the pot.

There are two phones, one in households on each of the troubled sides. And the phone call went like this:

"They had a party down at Bessie's house. There were a lot of people there, and you weren't invited!" And the struggle goes on.

Feud for Thought

What does it take to make a feud?

Only a word or two to become imbued

In one's own family or from even a friend.

And why does it never seem to end?

Was it just a misunderstanding?

And how did it ever get to be unending?

But the worse thing about all that,

People take sides in that ugly spat.

Beware of those who sit on the side

And stir the action when it would subside.

They feed off all the excitement caused

By mindless acts without applause.

So what can any person do?

Listen to the thoughts I have for you:

Stay out of it and be friends to all,

And watch what you say when you come to

call.

And never say that you were right,

Or speak of them when out of sight.

Just laugh and go about your way,

And pray it'll end the very next day.

The Brotherhood of Friends

In the years that I have been returning to the Rock, I have never met anyone who would not be your friend, if only you would ask. I have met people from all areas of Newfoundland, and I am well aware of my Americanism. Yet I have always been accepted with open arms, a handshake and a ready smile. Now I am no longer the stranger, but rather the friend.

One native that I particularly admire for his artistic works and for his dedication to saving the Newfoundland pony is Cliff George. He is truly a rare man. He combines artistic talent, academic achievement and rough good humor with the hard life of the rural homeowner, horse owner, boat owner and husband. And this prime example of Newfoundland can be multiplied over and over.

The most wonderful beauty of this island can be found over and over in her sons and daughters, and particularly in Cliff's paintings.

My Newfoundland Friend

I have a giant of a friend

Who dances to the colors in his head

And waltzes with arty spirits

And is always easily led,

Led to the beauty of nature

In man, woman, horse and life,

Painting not only serenity,

But also the pain and the strife.

The lay of the land and the lore of the sea

Are brought to life by his hand,

Derived by the ear and eye of his mind,

Is the picture of Newfoundland's land.

Witness his reflection in all his works,

And feel the artist's compassion,

For he is a champion of all the old ways,

For the pony, the people and nation.

Such is the man I know and admire,

Who was made in God's special forge.

Such is the man who gives of himself.

Such is my friend Clifford George.

Age

We all feel the sting of time. Time itself goes on forever and we are constantly running after it. But the beauty of this race is that we can look back and marvel at our progress along that track. There are milestones that we pass, and if we learn from them and go forward, that is all we can ask of ourselves.

Wishful Thinking

Time goes by so awfully fast,

And oh how I wish I could make it last.

There is so much I want to do,

It'll be a shame I won't get all through.

But if I were younger once again,

I'd live it over as a young man.

I'll probably make the same mistakes,

Even though I know just what it takes

To make my life a better place

And share my love with those I face,

At work or play on every day,

And let things happen as they may.

So forgive each and every sin.

I know I won't do them again.

But that's one plus for going back,
To know I'll get things back on track.

And as I progress again through life,
I'll know how to handle all the strife.
And so I'll be a better man,
And help all the others as I can.

These noble thoughts can't come true,
So this is what I'll have to do:
I'll live each day as if it's the best,
Until I take my final rest.

Recap

Tales, music and song, and incidents are indelible parts of any history. When we were in school, often these were attached to a date. In 2002 this happened, in 1902 this happened, in1802 this occurred, and so it goes. Often this was learned by rote and repetition. Did it serve a purpose? Yes. Did we learn from it? Probably we did. But family stories and songs are remembered and related not so much by the year but rather for the event. I now know of Joey Smallwood because of a little ditty. I know of Buchans and its people. I know the spirit of Saint Johns. I know some of the traditions, cultures, and personality that make up the native Newfoundlander. So if I were to recreate a history, I would write…

A Short Opinionated, Poetical, Historical Overview of Newfoundland

The Newfoundlander,

Whether young or wizened with graven face,

Among the nations of men,

Stands tall and strong in his place.

Created in a trinity

Of the land, the sea, and the sky,

Wherever he turns

Are visions of beauty to fill the eye.

From the craggy peaks

To the boggy barrens that ease the grounds,

Down to the rocky shore and cliffs,

This is the mystic isle the sea surrounds.

And to this land,

There came a multiplicity of men,

The horned Viking contrasted to the Irish harp,

And other lands' men became fledgling
fishermen.

The lilting song of the language,

Born from these various lands,

Made music in the ears of strangers,

But they could not understand.

They tried to study the meter,

And they tried to study the rhyme,

But they did not know the heart and soul of
them

Who lived in that bygone time.

And so it was that

This cauldron created a very special nation.

Each man for his own and yet all for each,

All free, strong, hardy and filled with

determination.

They were determined to survive

The climate, the struggles and the strife.

Either coupled or alone,

They were creating a new life.

They lived communally,

But banded together just as the native tribes.

They were making a history

To be told by ancients and scribes.

Rules and regulations

Soon replaced life's natural flow,

And the pace became more hectic,

As the towns began to grow.

The man of the city

Has become sly and sophisticated.

He's given up a heritage

And his troubles aren't abated.

They live on through the seasons

In houses of many hues,

As they compete with Mother Nature

By creating special views.

While most of the people are working,

There are some who'd rather not.

But everyone supports them,

No matter how ill fated is their lot.

And out in the hinterland,

Where most services were few,

The people existed on staples,

And still managed to make do.

The pony has been replaced

By four wheelers with their growl,

And in governmental palaces,

The lordly politicians howl.

"Just how should the country go?"

Is the most often queried question.

And from the many choices,

They chose tainted confederation.

Still today are rude mainlanders

That jest at the island men.

They try to gain advantage

In hopes of besting them.

Yet through all of life's adversities,

The Newfoundlander still finds joy.

He cries or smiles and sighs at wiles,

And says, "That's some good, eh, boy?"

He still shows the world the wonders

Of the rock called Newfoundland.

He still makes his life and history,

And to me he's simply grand.

About the Author

The author has experienced many adventures as a teacher, athletic coach and as an artistic director/founder of a children's theatrical house. His ear for stories has helped him write plays for children for his theater group, his church and his school classes. He has always written stories and poems, but this is his first attempt at publication. He wishes he could recapture his earlier romantic letters to share with a larger audience.